For Zoë, Lily and Neve, with love – M.D.
For Hannah (Cat-person) – C.S.

Craig Smith used gouache and pen and ink
for the illustrations in this book.

Kane/Miller Book Publishers, Inc.
First American Edition 2008
by Kane/Miller Book Publishers, Inc.
La Jolla, California

Originally published in Australia in 2007 by Working Title Press, Kingswood, SA

Text copyright (c) Mike Dumbleton 2007
Illustrations copyright (c) Craig Smith 2007

Library of Congress Control Number:
Printed and bound in China
1 2 3 4 5 6 7 8 9 10

ISBN: 978-1-933605-73-9

CAT

Written by Mike Dumbleton
Illustrated by Craig Smith

Cat.

Dog.

Dog.

Cat.

Tall tree.

Thank goodness for that!

Cat.

Mouse.

Mouse.

Cat.

Small hole.

Thank goodness for that!

Cat.

Sprinkler.

Sprinkler.

Cat.

High fence.

Thank goodness for that!

Cat.

Bird.

Bird.

Cat.

Flap.
Flutter.

Thank goodness
for that!

Bike.

Cat.

Bike.

Cat.

Ding! Ding!

Thank goodness for that!

Cat.   Milk.

Milk.

Cat.

Splish.
Splatter.

Thank goodness for that!

Cat.

Mat.

Mat.

Cat.

Safe and warm.

Thank goodness for that!